This book is dedicated to everyone in the world for having to deal with everyone else.

SIMON & SCHUSTER BOOKS FOR YOUNG READERS

An imprint of Simon & Schuster Children's Publishing Division

1230 Avenue of the Americas, New York, New York 10020

Copyright © 2018 by Lydecker Publishing, Inc.

SIMON & SCHUSTER BOOKS FOR YOUNG READERS is a trademark of Simon & Schuster, Inc.

For information about special discounts for bulk purchases, please contact Simon & Schuster Special Sales at 1-866-506-1949 or business@simonandschuster.com.

The Simon & Schuster Speakers Bureau can bring authors to your live event. For more information or to book an event,

contact the Simon & Schuster Speakers Bureau at 1-866-248-3049 or visit our website at www.simonspeakers.com.

Book design by Lucy Ruth Cummins

The text for this book was set in Grit Primer.

The illustrations for this book were rendered in ink and watercolor.

Manufactured in China

0118 SCP

First Edition

2 4 6 8 10 9 7 5 3 1

Library of Congress Cataloging-in-Publication Data

Names: Kaplan, Bruce Eric, author.

Title: Someone farted / Bruce Eric Kaplan.

Description: First Edition. || New York : Simon & Schuster Books for Young Readers, [2018] || Summary: A family outing

goes awry when someone farts but no one will admit to being the culprit.

Identifiers: LCCN 2016036134|| ISBN 9781481490634 (hardcover) || ISBN 9781481490641 (ebook)

Subjects: || CYAC: Flatulence—Fiction.

Classification: LCC PZ7.K128973 So 2018 || DDC [E]—dc23 LC record available at https://lccn.loc.gov/2016036134

Someone Farted
by
Bruce Eric Kaplan

SIMON & SCHUSTER BOOKS FOR YOUNG READERS

New York   London   Toronto   Sydney   New Delhi

One Saturday morning the Krupke family went to the supermarket to do their dreaded weekly food shopping.

They drove in silence,

until Sally said quietly,
without looking up from
her book,

"Someone farted."

Everyone took a whiff.

She was right.

"It wasn't me," said Vinnie.

The parents denied it
was them.

Everyone looked at Sally, who finally said,

"It definitely wasn't me!"

They all rolled down their windows.

But the smell kept getting worse and worse.

Clearly whoever it was, was still farting.

Which brought a new round of accusations and denials.

Their mother, prone to overreacting, said, "I think I'm going to faint."

Vinnie, prone to worrying, asked, "Is there any way it could kill us?"

The smell was still so, so bad.

Which only made them all more upset.

Their mother looked in her bag for something to make the smell go away.

All she found was some hand sanitizer, which she desperately started spraying everywhere.

"Owww!" Their father screamed because it got in his eyes.

He almost got into an accident.

A police officer pulled them over
and wanted to know what was wrong.

"Someone farted!"

everyone shouted.

Then the squabbling began once more.

Vinnie and Sally erupted into violence, throwing all the old junk in the backseat at each other,

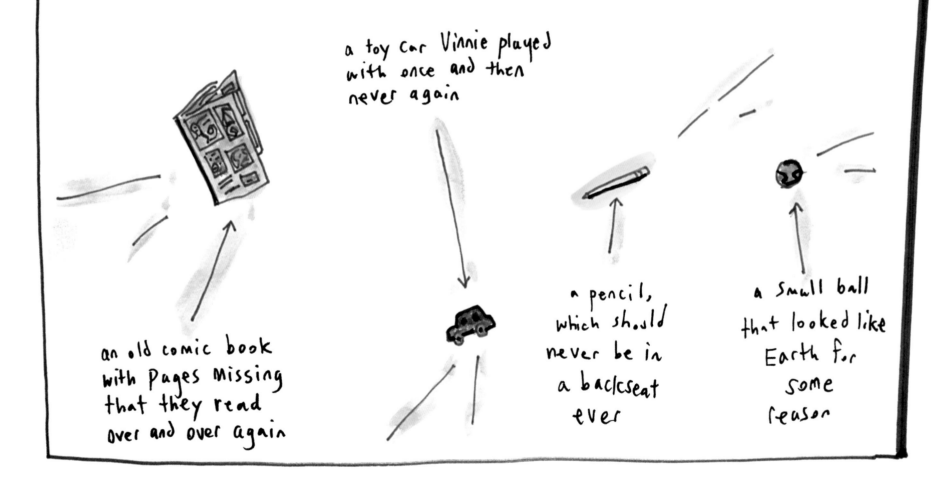

a toy car Vinnie played with once and then never again

an old comic book with pages missing that they read over and over again

a pencil, which should never be in a backseat ever

a small ball that looked like Earth for some reason

So they were arrested and brought downtown.

They were put in a cell

with a couple of kidnappers and some thieves.

One of the kidnappers wanted to know
what they were in for.

"Someone farted," Sally explained.
The kidnapper edged away from them nervously.

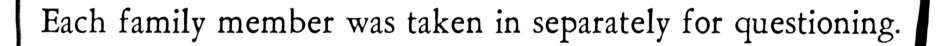

Each family member was taken in separately for questioning.

Not one of them admitted to the farting.

Back together in the cell they all started fighting again.

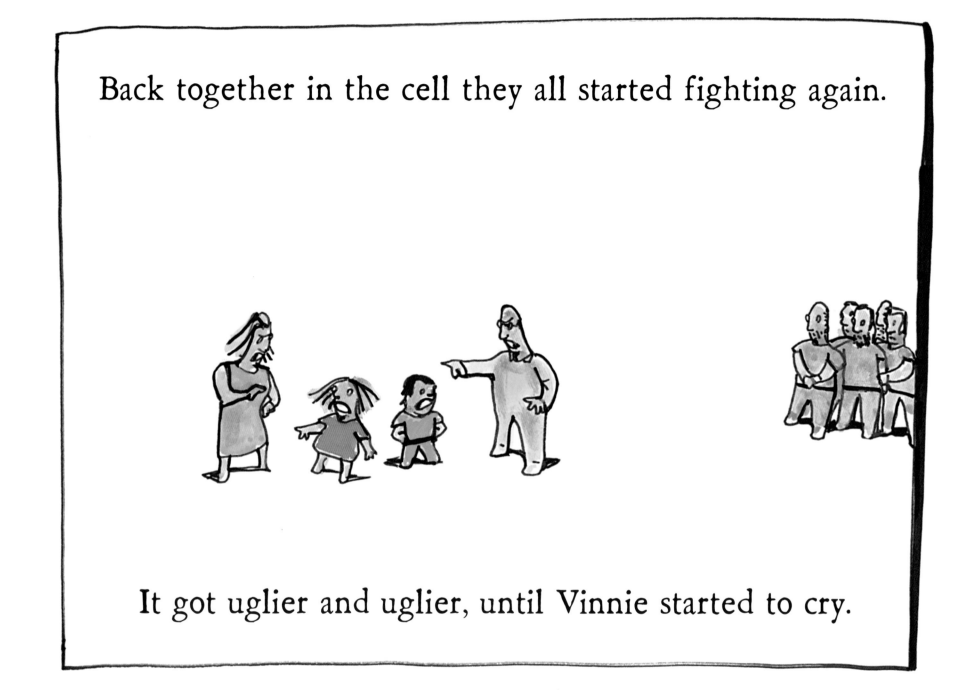

It got uglier and uglier, until Vinnie started to cry.

"Maybe it was me," he said.

"Maybe I was so involved with my book I didn't notice."

His parents looked at him, overcome with emotion.

His mother hugged him and said, "It was probably me."
Then his father said, "Maybe it was me."

Sally said, "Well, it definitely wasn't me."
Her parents shot her angry looks.

"She's lying," said one of the kidnappers.

Just then, they were taken to court
for disturbing the peace.

The judge was scary, like all judges.

But that didn't stop the father from giving an impassioned speech about blame and shame and love and family and, of course, farting.

The case was dismissed.

The Krupkes left jail triumphantly, determined to put this all behind them.

They were at peace, each one full of gratitude, and happy.

Until they realized they still needed
to do all of the boring things they did
every Saturday, starting with going to
the supermarket.